MW01298590

The New Book

Also by Nikki Giovanni

POETRY

Black Feeling Black Talk/Black Judgement

Re: Creation

My House

The Women and the Men

Cotton Candy on a Rainy Day

Those Who Ride the Night Winds

The Selected Poems of Nikki Giovanni

Love Poems

Blues: For All the Changes

Quilting the Black-Eyed Pea: Poems and Not Quite Poems

Acolytes

The Collected Poetry of Nikki Giovanni

Bicycles

Chasing Utopia

A Good Cry

Make Me Rain

PROSE

Gemini: An Extended Autobiographical Statement on My First Twenty-Five Years of Being a Black Poet

A Dialogue: James Baldwin and Nikki Giovanni

A Poetic Equation: Conversations Between Nikki Giovanni and Margaret Walker

Sacred Cows . . . and Other Edibles

Racism 101

Shimmy Shimmy Shimmy Like My Sister Kate: Looking at the Harlem Renaissance Through Poems

EDITED BY NIKKI GIOVANNI

Night Comes Softly: An Anthology of Black Female Voices

Appalachian Elders: A Warm Hearth Sampler

Grand Mothers: Poems, Reminiscences, and Short Stories About the Keepers of Our Traditions

Grand Fathers: Reminiscences, Poems, Recipes, and Photos of the Keepers of Our Traditions

100 Best African-American Poems

FOR CHILDREN

Spin a Soft Black Song

Vacation Time: Poetry for Children

Knoxville, Tennessee

The Genie in the Jar

The Sun Is So Quiet

Ego-Tripping and Other Poems for Young People

The Grasshopper's Song: An Aesop's Fable Revisited

Rosa

Abraham Lincoln and Frederick Douglass: An American Friendship

Hip Hop Speaks to Children

I Am Loved

The New Book

POEMS, LETTERS, BLURBS, AND THINGS

NIKKI
GIOVANNI

wm
WILLIAM MORROW
An Imprint of HarperCollins*Publishers*

HarperCollins books may be purchased for educational, business, or sales promotional use. For information, please email the Special Markets Department at SPsales@harpercollins.com.

hc.com

FIRST EDITION

Library of Congress Cataloging-in-Publication Data

Names: Giovanni, Nikki, author.
Title: The new book : poems, letters, blurbs, and things / Nikki Giovanni.
Description: First edition. | New York, NY : William Morrow, 2025. | Summary: "Nikki Giovanni's extraordinary final collection—a landmark of American literature—speaks to the fury of our current political moment while reflecting on the tragedies and triumphs of her early life"—Provided by publisher.
Identifiers: LCCN 2024061190 | ISBN 9780063447523 (hardcover) | ISBN 9780063447509 (ebook)
Subjects: LCGFT: Literature.
Classification: LCC PS3557.I55 N49 2025 | DDC 811/.54—dc23 /eng/20250528
LC record available at https://lccn.loc.gov/2024061190

ISBN 978-0-06-344752-3

25 26 27 28 29 LBC 5 4 3 2 1

Contents

ALL I REALLY HAVE

I am a poet
All I really have
Are words

I do have a dog
Who has all her shots
I have a home
In a neighborhood

I actually have about
Two dozen quilts
One of which the mother
Of a friend made
When she heard
I had cancer

I have a fishpond
Just gold fish
Though mother gold
Fish is very smart
She had four babies
Last summer
And made sure father
Gold fish nor birds
Ate them

A community of frogs
Lives there too
At first father frog
Would jump into the pond
When I came in the evening
To sit
Now he just looks
At me

And I tip
My glass of wine
To him
Both of us seeking rest

My home has a living
Room and a dining
Room
Though there are so many
Books we don't eat
Or sit there
We smile at our books
And I occasionally
Dust them

My windows are
Mostly stained glass
Two of which I
Found on auction
That once belonged
To a church built
By Slaves
I was lucky no
One else wanted
Them

One says
    60
A birthday present
From a dear
Thoughtful friend

The deck has been turned
Into a playpen
For the dog
Who always wants me
To grill

My den is friendly
Without a telephone
Though it has two
Desks and two
Chairs

My garden didn't
Do well last year
My green peppers came
But no okra
And the beautiful rosemary
Bush from Novella Nelson
Finally succumbed to winter
As did she

My car is 12 years old
And I want no other
I'm looking for a photo
Face shot
And this is not
A poem
Only some words
That define who I am

I am happy
And I love and embrace
What I love

WHY I'M THANKFUL

I'm thankful
Grandmother took me
to Sunday School
Now when I'm lonely
I have songs to sing

I'm grateful I can borrow
books from the library
Now when I sit in the hospital
I have another world to go to

I'm thankful I learned to cry
though I miss Mommy
She is no longer
in pain

I'm thankful She is in Heaven
with Grandmother
laughing and drinking a beer

I'm thankful
I understand Life
is not just fun
but also Duty

I go to school
Clean my room
Be nice to people

I'm thankful
I make them
Proud

YES

Sometimes everybody's coffee
Gets cold
And it's good to remember
All clocks tick
At a different time
No matter how close they are
To each other

Dogs snift
Each other
In community talk we call gossip
That cats
Run away from when they are unsure of you

We eat bullfrogs
And ride horses
Sometimes we pray
For rain
Sometimes
For sun

We are born
We will die

Sometimes
That's a good
Idea
To understand

WON'T YOU BE MY NEIGHBOR?

While the sky was that sort of gray . . . not quite light . . . you could hear the birds . . . begin to sing

Since the puppy needs to go out . . . at that hour . . . I am up . . . watching the little birds . . . go off to hunt . . . for food

There is a copper sculpture on the railing . . . which I hadn't realized holds . . . Mother Wren's eggs . . . the puppy ballet dances at it . . . since she knows . . . something alive is in there

The puppy only wants to play with the babies . . . like the Cincinnati Gorilla only wanted to play with the little boy though the humans didn't understand that . . . and shot him . . . soon the puppy will have to go to the kennel . . . until the baby Wrens learn to fly . . . maybe only a week or two . . . since she . . . too . . . doesn't want to hurt anything . . . only to get to know them better

I go inside and make my breakfast . . . It is spring . . . and the blue is brighter . . . the big birds are waking up

And I have to hurry . . . to take ten pills . . . because my neurologist two years ago sent a letter to the DMV saying I should not drive . . . but has "forgotten" to send the notice that now I can . . . Luckily I have friends to help out . . . though every time I have to ask for a ride . . . I am angry all over again . . . Oh my doctor says I'm sorry I forgot . . . Maybe I am close to hating him

But the sky is bright blue . . . and the birds are singing . . . and I am ready for my ride . . . to work

We drive down the hill and wait for the traffic to make room to embrace us . . . I hope we turn right even though we will pass our neighbor who flies the confederate flag . . . you would think the fascist would learn by now . . . They Will Never Win . . . they lost the Civil War . . . WWI . . . WWII . . . and all the others no matter how vicious fascists are . . . One day I will picket him . . . with a banner that says LOSER . . . just in case . . . he and they forgot they . . . LOST

My day would start with anger . . . except we reach the ramp where Roanoke Street turns to 460 . . . where a pigeon family lives . . . How they like the rhythm of cars over their head . . . I don't know . . . but I always hope to get a red light . . . so that father pigeon can wave . . . at me . . . and I can smile . . . back

Up we go to the first turn . . . Starbucks . . . on both sides of the corner . . . nests in the "b" . . . which customers complain about but most of us love them . . . the other corner is FedEx where the "d" makes room for a home . . . again I smile . . . because of the coffee . . . and my friends in their nests

Luckily I don't have a job . . . I have a career . . . the third floor has the best people and we can gossip a bit . . . my students make me smile . . . I hate the telephone . . . and don't know how to email . . . but I lunch and watch the green trees from both my windows . . . and the birds who swoop by . . . to say hello

My ride home is ready . . . and so am i

Dinner is early . . . I grill . . . Ginney makes veggies . . . she does dishes . . . I clean the grill

Then the best part of the day . . . a glass of champagne on the deck . . . to watch the birds come home

Little birds first . . . while we talk . . . bigger birds with the second glass . . . the sky is turning dark blue . . . the moon is a crescent smiling

Then the dark

I don't know what the birds' names are . . . I know the robin because of the blue eggs . . . I know the hawk because we met when the puppy came to live with us . . . she thought about a meal for her babies and I had a strong talk with her . . . I don't bother her babies . . . she doesn't bother mine . . . we are both happy now . . . the tree limbs bend over the fishpond so the bigger birds don't see the goldfish . . . I don't know the names of the bigger birds either but they wave on their way to bed

It is night now . . . we sit quietly . . . we soon will hear the bats take off

It's not that late but the news is on . . . and the mosquitoes . . . moths . . . and other flying insects are out

We go in . . . humming a tune . . . Won't You Be My Neighbor?

FEAR

Eat In or Take Out?

I think fear should be a spice. Something we sprinkle on our steaks just before we put them on the grill; something we mix in with our corn muffins and bake at 350 degrees for twenty minutes or until golden brown. Maybe we take fear leaves to decorate our apple pie right out of the oven . . . hot before or the leaves will burn and not look nearly so pretty. I'm thinking if we can learn to distill fear we have two wonderful preparations: perfume for smells and alcohol for ingestion.

Perfume carries its own scent of danger and excitement but when we throw a little *Fear* in there things really heat up. Ask John Edwards or Herman Cain and see if I'm not right. *Fear: The Scent He Can't Resist*. We'd have to find an exclusive outlet for it. We wouldn't want everybody to be able to get their hands on it. I'll have to form a committee to find that solution. Maybe the White House has some ideas. Or . . . oh yes . . . The Tiger Woods Emporium! *Get Your Fear Right Here*. You can practice your swing, whatever that might mean, while your bottle is bagged.

And if we made it drinkable we'd probably have a light green liquid with its own two-ounce top. You can take your fear on the rocks . . . or slip a bit of Coke in there to make it mighty smooth. We could get the Culinary Channel to feature fear at one of the drink offs and we'd reward the best new barrister with his/her very own gold bottle of fear to be used anytime they'd like.

I need to explain right here, it's not fear that causes problems, it's when hatred is combined with it. Fear on its own tells you not to lend your cousin money; don't go down that dark street, girl; take yourself home from this party now. Fear is a warning signal. Healthy. Good idea. That fish smells funny. My dog does not like this man. Fear is a good thing. It's why I want to keep it exclusive.

If everyone can have fear then we have to cut it. Like drugs. It's not the cocaine that kills you it's the stuff they cut it with to make the drugs go further. You don't want pure fear but you don't want it cut with hatred either. Hatred is a bad idea. Which is why it's cheap and available anywhere you look.

Maybe what will really work is we all need to have a fear tree in our backyard or a small fear plant growing on our apartment windowsill. When we are feeling uneasy we pluck a few leaves and find the right place to put them. Champagne would be the number one choice but spaghetti works, too. Have a little fear at least once a week and you will build up your resistance. Like a vaccination. Then when wars and hatreds come along you'll be able to recognize that's just another expression of fear. No thanks, I've had my quota.

That's what I'm thinking we really need: An Antidote for Fear.

TONI MORRISON

I wish I owned a restaurant then I could run Specials: Today Toni Morrison stew. An exotic mix of tears and sympathy. Nothing grows except The Bluest eyes and a special shot of Pecola which flies over very quickly because no one can really embrace the fear and hatred. The best thing about The Bluest Eye special is the Marigolds. They didn't flower but the seeds are there. Drop a few in the bowl and see what grows. Or doesn't.

I also really recommend the Sula. The mixture of two girlfriends who lose each other. It does not come with dessert but it can have hot bread. When the Nel is ready to be taken out of the oven that's the best time to put the Sula in the refrigerator. Timing is everything with this dish. It has to balance the desire with the impossible. Sometimes the chef will put a bit of college in to mix with that wonderful hat. The hat is a lot of fun because whoever catches it gets a free Song of Solomon and a fresh glass of milk.

Of course we'd mix Jazz Belovedly with a movie and a talk or two. Let's call it The Morrison Café. Vodka, though my preference is cheap champagne. And only bottled water.

If Toni's home had been open to gourmets there would always be porgies frying. Yeah sure everyone thinks fried food is bad for your heart or something but how did the Black Americans get through slavery and segregation without catfish and chittlins? Porgies were a treat. There was a restaurant in The Village that sometimes had porgies and knowing Toni loved them I would go to New York and pick her up. It was more than a poet could actually afford but she was, after all, Toni Morrison. I had my car take me up to her home and take us to the café. I still don't know what we talked about but when dinner was over I would ride back to her house. She always said she could call her own car but I knew my grandmother would have a heavenly fit if I let Toni go home alone.

So I rode up said Good Night and came back to Manhattan. She must have known poets are poorer than novelists but she also knew we both were southerners and there were rules.

I didn't ever know the home that burned down but what I loved about the home on the Hudson was the Nobel Prize citation in the downstairs bathroom. I am fortunate to call Toni Morrison friend. Mostly neither of us had much to say. There was always a comfortable silence when I visited her. My mother transitioned 24 June then my sister 5 August of the same year. I tried to do what any good daughter and sister would do and I think I got it done. But it was sad. One afternoon I was sitting at my desk just sort of being dismayed when I decided to call Toni. I probably talked more than ever and she was kind enough to listen. She finally said Nikki, Write. That's all you can do. Write.

I wish I had a restaurant then I could also cook up a special Morrison Stew to help us all go through this. The title is The Last Interview but there will never be a last interview with Toni. Her books live and talk to us. She could have said Read. But she said Write. And she is Right.

WAITING FOR JASON

I feel
The sun
But I look
At the moon

I watch
The clouds dance
Across the clear blue sky

I sing a love song
To the twinkling stars

A mountain brook
Babbles while ivy
Holds tight

The oak tree rocks
New born owls
To sleep

And I sit
With patches of cloth
And snickles of cake
And just a little bit
Of cold red wine

Waiting for Jason
To come home

FOR SCOTT

Dear Scott:

I know where you are . . . out in the clouds somewhere with me. Earth is so foolish right now that it's a good idea to try Mars or even Pluto if you are brave. Those folk shooting unarmed men and sleeping women are not brave they are cowardly fools. Your students are lucky to have you when you come back in our galaxy to teach with them. I remember cooking for you all but you can't do that now because of the virus so I guess the next best thing is singing for them. Or maybe you should have them sing for you. My students and I sang this year and they learned you do not have to have a good voice to sing. Plus my question to them was: if you sing who or what will answer. Hippos came to me and I was so happy because they are big and strong and they took good care of me. Other students had birds which sang them to sleep. Or maybe if you are not very careful you will be with me having a glass of beer and your students will be sad because they are too young to drink. I know, I know, they will think they can sneak and drink but sneaking is cheating and cheating is so trumpish and nobody wants to whine like that. So I'm inviting you to visit with me at Mars. I'll have you back by Monday and you can tell your students that the Earth is as round as their heads. Or their grandmother's biscuits. Or the dreams they dream as they float off to sleep. Your former teacher, Nikki

THE LONGEST WAY ROUND

Mommy taught
3rd grade
Her book was The Longest
Way Round (Is The Shortest Way Home)

I was an adult
Before i realized
How True

Their marriage
Is none of your business
You don't understand
Your parents don't owe
You anything
You finally say to yourself:
They Have Nothing
I want
Except
I remember this Blue Book
With a wonderful title
My Mother West Wind Stories
And Mommy singing
Time After Time

It worked
I am Happy

THE STERLING SILVER MIRROR

(For DePaul University)

No matter how the wind and the stars carried the news
The slaves knew
Sherman was coming
All they had to do was wait:
As they sang the Spiritual "Why Can't I Wait on the Lord?"
They had the patience to know He may not come
When you call Him
But He always comes on time

My great-great-grandmother was a slave holding inside
Her the first of our family to be born
Free
Sherman came burning the hate
And greed freeing my ancestors
My great-great-grandmother who had never seen her own face
Carried her free baby and a sterling silver hand mirror away

Cornelia whom we called MamaDear was the first
To be born free

MamaDear married Watson and birthed
Three sons and a daughter
MamaDear gave her youngest son the sterling silver mirror
When he graduated from Fisk University

We forget the enslaved had no way of knowing
What they looked like except through the eyes of those who loved them
The men had no shoes to wear other than their feet became leather
Both were precious
Grandpapa had shoes and the mirror

Some in the family say
The mirror was stolen
But how can you steal when you were

When I left my parents' home I was the youngest daughter I took only
Two things:
A diamond pendant Sister Althea gave me for eighth grade graduation
And The Sterling Silver Hand Mirror
I am 81 years old: I have both still

THE COAL CELLAR

Electricity was late and expensive
Coming to Appalachia
Knoxville especially so
Twice a month the coal
Man would come to fill the cellar
For warmth and sometimes food
And what I loved most was the fireplace
Where Grandmother and Grandpapa would sit
Near to tell stories but
Oak Ridge came for the War
Or maybe the War came for Oak Ridge
And atomic energy replaced coal
And the cellar became a home for mice
And maybe some insects which we never
Needed to bother since they didn't bother us

One summer day Grandmother said
To me "Since John Brown will be gone
For the Conference why don't we see what
Is in the Cellar"
I didn't think anything but if your grandmother
Asks you to go cellaring with her
You go

Way to the front she pulled a box out
And handed it to me
"See? I thought it would still be here"
And we climbed out and up or maybe up and out
And into the kitchen where we were both dripping
With ash
"This belongs to your great-grandmother
Cornelia
The first person born free"

And there was a sterling silver dinner spoon and fork
Black as can be but properly hallmarked

"I'll let you polish them"

Which I did though it took
Several days
To bring them to silver

I'll bet there are many precious
Things in the cellars
Of Appalachia
The most being the trust my grandmother
Had in me to keep the silver polished
And not discussed with anyone

Maybe not a big bank account or trust fund
And certainly not any property but I inherited
A morning and a great deal of knowledge
In a cold coal cellar
With my grandmother

THE BUS DIDN'T STOP

Running running running
The rain was at my back
the wind was pushing me
I didn't want to fall
But the bus was coming

I needed to cross the street
Curbs were splashing
Maybe the cars would want to stop
But what if they didn't see me

There was a green light
I hit the crosswalk
Damp and cold
But the bus was not going to stop

Then I stood
Wet dripping
On my walk to class

Then quiet
Darkness
An explosion
So hard everyone
Covered
Their ears
Then the running
The bodies flying
Bags flying
Screams

The sidewalk folk running
To help
"Honey, Honey," my mother called
"Wake up or you'll be late"

I sat straight up
Then
Turned over

READING OTHER PEOPLE'S POEMS

Seeing a line
Or an image
A metaphor
Or maybe just a dream
I read other people's
Poetry
And wonder
Why
Didn't I think
Of that

Not in envy
Nor judgment
Just something
To do
Until the oatmeal
arrives

VOTE

(2020)

It's not a hug
Nor mistletoe at Christmas

It's not a colored egg
At Easter
Nor a bunny hopping
Across the meadow

It's A Vote

Saying you are
A citizen

Though it sometimes
Is chocolate
Or sometimes vanilla
It can be a female
Or a male
It is right
Or left
I can agree
Or disagree but
And this is an important but
I am a citizen

I should be able
To vote from prison
I should be able
To vote from the battlefield
I should be able
To vote when I get a driver's license

I should be able
To vote when I can purchase a gun
I must be able
To vote
If I'm in the hospital
If I'm in the old folks' home
If I'm needing a ride
To the Polling Place

I am a citizen

I must be able to vote

Folks were lynched
Folks were shot
Folks' communities were gerrymandered
Folks who believed
In the Constitution were lied to
Burned out
Bought and sold
Because they agreed
All Men Were Created Equal

Folks vote to make us free

It's not cookies
Nor cake
But it is the icing
That is so sweet

Good for the Folks
Good for Us

RAISE YOUR HAND

(In Favor of Immigrants)

how many of you sitting
here
think some woman of color
Black Brown Yellow White
woke up this morning thinking
"Goooolly . . . I can go to the airport
and clean toilets?"

Raise your right hand

how many of you sitting here
woke up this morning thinking
How lucky can they be
Oh Lordy I wish I could
do that

Raise your left hand

how many of us sitting
here gave one dollar
to those women knowing
they are underpaid
and not appreciated
at all

Raise either hand

did you know if we all
gave one dollar
every time we urinated
those women might
take 100 dollars home

to feed their mother
their children
their uncle who moved in with them
their husband who will beat them

Raise any hand

how many of you
when you see those women
say thank God
it's not me

Raise both your motherfucking hands
and Clap

PRIVATE SECRETS

(Like or No Like)

Maybe there is no
Problem

We are watched only

the question is
in or out
of jail

We have no secrets
since the world shrunk
the icebergs melted
and all the year books
are digitized

president trump measures
his dick size
though not the size
of his heart
and we press Like
or No Like
as if it mattered

We are born
with someone but
no matter
the obituary
or the eulogy
We die
alone

press Like
or No
Like

You are your own
Private
Your own
Secret
Your own
Life

Press Like
Or
No Like

It's your face
Book
Tweet

MARCH ON WASHINGTON 10TH ANNIVERSARY

Let's recognize the obvious:

If you want money
You've got to work

If you want sex
You've got to love

When you need community
You have to commit

If you want freedom
You've got to struggle

Some things will never
Change

Life is about
The living

LOOK

(Something May Be There)

I go down
My mountain
Five miles an hour because
A mother chipmunk was running
Across the street
To take food
To her babies

I'm a black woman
I run
Across corners too
To feed my son
And granddaughter
And I don't want
Them hit
Because some one
Was not looking

We are Earthlings
On the same planet
In the same Galaxy
Waiting for an Alien
To come show me
How to make biscuits

I already know
How
To fry chicken wings

A PRAISE SONG FOR *ROOTS* BY ALEX HALEY

I was born in Tennessee in the old Knoxville General Hospital. I was the first person in my family born in a hospital. When my sister and cousins and I would argue they would say "You don't even belong to us." I don't think I believed them but I did look at my family in a different way, sort of. I knew they were just being mean but I also thought Well, What if they're right? What if I was picked up by accident? What if I belonged to someone else?

We moved from Knoxville to Woodlawn, Ohio, which is north of Cincinnati. This was during the age of segregation. My mother and father had jobs which had not been possible in Knoxville. We rented a two-bedroom house: kitchen, sitting room and we had an outhouse. I remember the outhouse and for reasons I don't understand have a fondness of that memory. In fact, when I bought my own home I had Dan make an outhouse out front to collect my mail. It's a sentimental thing.

We were poor. That's understood. When my parents saved enough money to purchase a home in Lincoln Heights, a segregated community just outside Cincinnati, we all felt we were big stuff. Lincoln Heights didn't have garbage collection so we had to burn our garbage. I loved it. The lot next door was empty and I remember the rabbits lived over there. Probably other things, too. I would chase the rabbits but I was never successful. I only wanted to play with them but they didn't understand that. I guess all they knew about me was that I burned garbage every night. I would stand and watch the fire. I don't think I worried so much about burning the house down as I was simply fascinated by fire. Some evenings I watched the moon. Mostly I remember just dreaming.

Mommy taught third grade at St. Simon's School. Gus, my father, taught math at Lincoln Heights Middle School. One day, for reasons totally unknown or not remembered, I decided to meet Gus who walked up the hill every day to our home. I had a blue bike. As I started down the hill I seem to remember or thought I heard Gus say "Look at that crazy kid coming down the hill." By that time the bike was actually riding me. I still, at 72, have scars from that.

But I survived.

I'm trying to understand my father. A part of me thinks he was mean; a part thinks he drank too much; a part just doesn't understand. But every Saturday night about 11:00 p.m. if you asked what I was doing I was hearing my father beat my mother. The saddest sound I ever heard one night was "Gus, please don't hit me." It was a prayer. I had an older sister but she was always friendly. She had girlfriends that she would spend the weekend with. She would come home Sunday late and talk about what a good time she had. I am not friendly. I stayed home. Until I couldn't stay anymore. My God-Mother, Baby West, died and left me $50. I walked to the bank in Lockland to see what I could do with it. I could take it, they said. I purchased a Butterfinger and a ticket to Knoxville. Our neighbor, Mr. Gray, who must surely have known what went on in our home, gave me a ride to the train station.

Grandmother must have known what I was trying to get away from yet we never even discussed it. I asked if I could stay with them. She and Grandpapa didn't hesitate: Yes.

I read now about the need for Black boys to have fathers in the home and I wonder. White boys have fathers at home and they end up in the KKK. The white boys end up calling us names. Spitting at us and worse. Now the white boys are policemen shooting unarmed 14-year-olds to death. Or they are billionaires running for President. Stirring up hate. I'm not sure fathers are necessary beyond their biological function. If we are going to criminalize women for abortions shouldn't we also criminalize the men who impregnated them?

But we have a larger question. Alex said we have Roots. He traced his back to Africa. What I really understand about my Roots is that the Black woman mated, whether willfully or not, with the life form that was on this land they were brought to. No matter its Color, Race or Religion. That life form would now like to deny its responsibility. But the Black woman loved that which she incubated. And, for the most part, brought it forth to believe in the future. Alex did a good job. He reminded us of hope. All I'm saying is that everything has Roots. Our only question is do we pull them up like weeds to be destroyed or do we nurture them to allow them to blossom. I knew Alex. He gave us, at a perilous time, reasons to go forth. He reminded us, we all have Roots. Our human, our humane, job is to entwine and enrich.

MY CONTRACT WITH AMERICA

(Or Is That America's Contract on Negroes?)

You can't lie
To a liar
Or steal from a thief
Or out run an AR-15
Nor escape from a burning Boeing

We all know Jesus won't
Come
When you call Him
But He always comes
On time
So why can't we wait
On the Lord

My supermarket hates me
Just because every now and then
I take something
Forgetting to pay
A light bulb here a Coca-Cola there
Sometimes lemonade for the kids
A beer for mother

I seldom take meat though sometimes
Bread
There is a lot of it anyway

And fruit will spoil
If I don't eat it

White folks feel
The same way
So I don't take anything
From them

I give my song
My dance
I give laughter
And show them how
To make quilts
Out of patches they throw away

I am not scared
Of them

If they would stay
On their side of the street
I would be happy

They are scared of me

They want me
To be like them
And learn to hate
And fear
And wear hoods over their faces

Or badges
Over their hearts

I want to be
Proud of me
And keep on
Walking
Down the street
Across the bridge
Sitting on my bus seat
Paid an equal pay

And keep on loving

RE: MOVEON'S LOVE LETTER TO ESSENTIAL WORKERS

Education is a dream
Or perhaps a dream is education
But a clean building with a smiling teacher
A grocery shelf with our favorite foods
Soap lotion and Flonase too
Trash picked up and taken away
The wave of the postwoman who delivers our magazines
These are dreams too
And when we awake we must find the song
That has a happy beat
That says thanks thanks thanks for all you do
For all of us
Bebop de bop
We thank you
A lot

VOTE 2024

(It Matters)

At sometime
There has to be something
Called thinking

At sometime
There has to be something
Called courage

At sometime
There has to be Black
Men who step up recognizing
They are needed

They were needed
In slavery

They were needed
to destroy segregation
They are needed
To vote for Harris

They are needed
To understand ice cubes blow west and are not for us

Vote for Harris

Find the courage
To help rid us all
    Of the festering mold in the white house

Vote like your grandmother would be proud of you

Vote because you like to say: “It ain’t mine”
But if not that then another
Vote because men
Vote for the future

Vote because you are not a coward
Vote because you know we need you to
step up biden your time
because you are a citizen
Vote. We need you brother
Vote for the love we gave you last night
Vote for the best in you
Vote

VINES

My mother died
13 or 14 years
Ago

I took the flowers
Home
And put most in
Water
The gift of life

They sit by the window
In the sunnyside
Of my bedroom
And the roots
Have taken hold

Sometimes a leaf
Will yellow
And I pull it off

It is dead

And there must be
Room
For a new leaf

Things that are dead
Cannot be saved

My mother will always
Live in my heart

All nazis must be
Picked
And thrown
away

SOME CHRISTMAS QUESTIONS AND ONE ANSWER

Who needs to understand Billionaire is the most unnecessary thing on Earth? You Do.

Who needs to know there can be no joy nor pleasure just because there is power and money?
You Do.

Who needs to know Health is the one personal thing that doesn't belong to you? You Do.

Who needs to insist Water should be pure: Air should be clean: animals should have parks to live and breed in? You Do.

Who needs to vote that senators and representatives can only serve as long as the president? You Do.

Who needs to understand the folk we put in office should not be paid more than the folk who put them there? You Do.

Who needs to quit being afraid of folk who have different colored skin: who worship God differently: who speak another language: love another or the same person: You Do.

Who needs to think why Prince Harry is marrying a Black woman who if he had tried to marry her a few years ago the Queen would not allow it? Edward VIII couldn't marry a white American divorcée: Margaret couldn't marry Peter Townsend, but Harry can do a bunch of things. What does the Queen have in mind? Maybe that Rule Britannia should be more than a song so the fifth in line marries a Black American divorcée and everyone is happy. Who needs to think how long will it be before the Crown reaches out to the Gay community? You Do.

I remember when irons got hot enough to scorch clothes, telephones were on something called a party line and there were signs that said Colored and White. Do You?

But mostly who is ready to concede when another life form visits us that we are not from the United States in North America or France in Europe or China in Asia or Ghana in Africa or any country or continent but Earth? You Do.

There is some joy and reason in the meeting of Europe and Africa that we have not explored.

Who needs to pay our teachers and graduate students so that we can explore that relationship. You Do.

It is time to move on to the twenty-first century. Who needs to be brave enough to go forward and save our Democracy? We are. Maybe.

Merry Christmas and a Happy New Year.

THE NATURE CONSERVANCY

The Nature Conservancy
4245 Fairfax Drive
Suite 100
Arlington, VA 22203

7 January 2021

Dear Nature Conservatory:

I am not wealthy though I do contribute what I can to you and especially what I can for the birds. I am surprised that you and the other nature societies have not bonded together to ask the Rockefeller Center to cease cutting old tall trees down. This year, as you are aware, an Owl was nesting in the tree. Fortunately it was saved but it, like the young people on our borders trying to have a better life, cannot go home again. Even if someone was willing to return it to the place where the tree was killed the Owl would still not have a family to teach it and help it grow.

It seems with as much plastic as there is in the trash there could be made a tree as tall as Rockefeller Center would like. They could have a contest or something to help the trash go to better use and leave the birds and trees to do their job of restoring the earth.

I sincerely hope you will consider letting the trees and its family live and put the plastic to work.

Sincerely,
Nikki Giovanni

A KEYNOTE ADDRESS

Poetry Is A Trestle. In this keynote we will explore the questions: How does poetry help us understand the development of language and the changing of language help us explore the development of history? We look to poetry for emotional and scientific newness. Poems create the idea and the necessity of a new world. From Earth's oldest language, which we have now sent on two CDs to Mars, to our youngest, Rap, poems have evolved to hope and correct that which recognizes what does not exist but what may exist if we find new words to embrace. From Hindu to Christianity to other Gods and philosophies we look to poetry to carry us over. There is a bridge which we will walk over to tomorrow. **Poetry is our trestle.**

SERENA

Even at my age understanding what love is, is difficult. I'm a baby sister, too, and I remember watching my big sister be able to do everything. They used to tease me: Nikki can you read? No but Gary can. Nikki can you play the piano? No but Gary can. Nikki can you dance? No but Gary can. And I was so proud that I had a big sister who could do all the important things. I wonder if Serena felt just the opposite.

I wonder if Serena sat on the side of the court and watched her big sister play tennis. I wonder if she was saying to herself I'm going to do that. Serena was the little girl watching the rabbit run down the rabbit hole. There were other sisters who she could have emulated but she chose this one. And I have to think this one chose her.

I watched the first time they played each other in a tournament. The reporter kept asking Who will win? And Venus calmly and coolly said A Williams. Venus not only won but she also showed her baby sister how to win. Don't let them push you around. I recently watched Venus play Coco and I said to myself: Venus is teaching Coco how to win, too. Not by the score but by how you carry yourself. Having a big sister who loves you enough to be your teacher is great.

Wheaties is wonderful to have Serena on the box cover. I purchased four boxes to be framed for my granddaughter and myself and friends. I want that box cover hanging from every wall in the kitchen. But it is Venus who has really taught them all.

Sure, Serena has 23 championships and we are all so proud of her. We watched her be robbed of her 24th though that will come. Serena has shown us you can be a woman with attitude and muscles. You can learn to speak four languages. You can take the body that used to stand on an auction block and put it on the cover of *Vanity Fair* naked, pregnant, proud. And you can put that same body on the cover of *Harper's Bazaar* wrapped in gold. You can be *Sports Illustrated*'s Best Dressed with your green high heels and a smirk and find someone you love to share making a baby with. Little Olympia is lucky, though, to have Aunt Venus to show her running down the rabbit hole to meet the Queen isn't all it's cracked up to be.

We give what we can. The Hare gave her speed to help her friend the Turtle feel better about herself. The poets give our words to say what we admire. Serena gives us a new woman to say we are not afraid of our bodies or our minds. She had a big sister to say Don't be afraid of yourself. We are all lucky for big sisters. And baby sisters who listen.

GIRL TALK

(Lyrics)

We watch the fireflies
Go home to bed
The sun is setting
But the moon has not
Yet shown her hand
We sit on mother's porch
So glad to hear the birds sing
And wait to see the lovely bats
Begin their evening wing
We smile
And hold each other's hand
And toast our champagne glasses
We know it's love time
Our time

FLOATING

I'm always interested
In my dreams
When I awake
Sometimes I'm holding
Hands with a former lover
Sometimes a future one
Usually I'm sitting
By the window
Watching the raindrops
Fall

I wish I could
Ride them back up
Bouncing on top
Twirling around
Wrapped in a bubble
Cloud
No thunder
No lightning
Just me
With you
Just floating down
A solo river
Humming a love song
dreaming

THE THREE RIDERS

It was just beginning to be dawn. The sky was turning a light blue but there seemed to be gray clouds coming. "Honey, honey, wake up," Edna Bunny called. "There is a big storm coming. Al Roker says it will hit tomorrow. Get up. You've got a problem." Bobby Bunny turned over. He kicked the quilt off and rubbed his eyes. "What do you mean?" "A big storm is coming and will hit us about tomorrow at noon. Roker says it's coming straight up the coast." Bobby jumped to his feet. "Oh No! If that happens I won't be able to deliver the Easter Eggs. Oh my! What should I do?" Edna had made him a strong breakfast of grits with lots of butter, wheat toast with strawberry jam and a pot of coffee. "Eat your breakfast and think," she advised. "Do you think it's just water?" "No. Roker says it's bringing snow. He's advising everybody to get what they need to be able to stay in for a couple of days!" "Oh, Edna. I have to get out. I have Easter Eggs to hide for the children. I can't let them down." "Well, who do we know who can move around in snowy weather?" Bobby thought for only a minute. "Santa. Maybe he can help me." Edna looked worried. "How will you get to the North Pole? You know they won't answer the phone until Spring." "I'll have to run up. It will only take a day." But Edna still looked worried about him being caught in the storm. "Why don't you call Pete Pusitanile? Maybe he can help with the underground railroad." "Great idea!" and he got on the phone right away.

Pete like most of the groundhogs was asleep but the phone rang and rang until it awoke him. Pete was a bit grumpy but Bobby explained the problem. Pete agreed. The children had to have their eggs. "Come to the big oak tree," Pete instructed. "I'll let you in." Bobby wrapped up, kissed his wife, and hopped as fast as he could to the oak tree. Pete was there with a lunch bag. "My wife thought you would need something to eat. It's a long trip. Almost a day. I've called ahead. All the doors will be open. Turn Left at each door. Rest about the fourth door. Eat lunch then turn Left. Watch out for roots." Bobby hugged Pete. "Thanks, Pete. Thanks a lot." Then off he hopped.

At each turn he turned Left. He rested as he was instructed. Then hopped off again. The groundhog underground was working to make it faster and easier. Then he saw a sign. QUICKEST WAY TO THE NORTH POLE. It was a right turn. Bobby looked at it and was tempted but he said to himself: Follow the instructions. And turned Left.

It was just turning dark when he emerged at the North Pole. He was tired and very thirsty but he had gotten there. He arrived at Santa's house knocking on the front door.

Santa and Mrs. Claus heard the knocking and he thought a branch had fallen against the house. They knew a storm was coming but they were surprised it had arrived so quickly. Sarah Claus said, "No. I think it's somebody." She put down her knitting and went to open the door. "My goodness. What a surprise. Come in. Come in. Santa! Look who's here." Santa leaned forward with a big smile. "EB! What are you doing here this time of the year? You've got work to do Tomorrow!" Bobby came into the living room. The fireplace felt really good. Then he noticed Santa's foot. "What happened to your foot?" "Oh it was stupid of me. I was around the Naughty List just making sure, you know, when I saw this bourbon, 1865, siting on the table. Now Everyone knows Mitch and his family have been on the Naughty List since my great-grandfather but an 1865 represents Freedom and, well, I couldn't resist. I slid down the chimney but my foot got caught on the way up. Thank Goodness Rudolph gave me light, and a couple of mice pushed a brick, and I was able to get back on the sleigh. But I had broken my foot."

Easter Bunny was sad. Santa couldn't help.

Sarah brought a bowl of carrot soup in for Bobby. "I called your wife to tell her you're all right." Bobby was grateful for both.

"I don't know what I'll do. The children need their Easter Eggs and I'm not going to be able to give them." "Wait a minute," Sarah said. "I can help. I think Rudolph is still here. Maybe he can drive the sleigh. I know the route. I've watched Santa all these years. Let's call Rudolph."

Rudolph and David had just sat down for dinner. When they heard Sarah's voice Ruddy said, "I'll be right there." David promised to keep dinner hot. Ruddy was at the door in five minutes. Bobby and Sarah explained the problem. But Sarah thought it only fair to remind Rudolph that they respected his plans. "David and I were going to Copenhagen tomorrow for the reindeer edition of The Christmas Story. We were going over to see some friends but the opera isn't until two more days. The kids must have their eggs. If we're going, though, we need to leave no later than midnight because we're going to run into the storm." Sarah and Bobby thanked Ruddy. Off he went to get the sleigh ready. "Don't forget to bundle up! It's going to be really wet and cold."

When Rudolph got home he told David the problem. David insisted Ruddy eat a good dinner then they both went to get the sleigh ready. Sarah bundled up very tightly, and Bobby and EB, as Santa called him, put on Santa's coat and hat. When Rudolph pulled up they were ready.

First we have to go to the chickens to get the eggs. They told me they are ready. Then we have to turn North and Northeast to deliver. Going down was cold but smooth. The chickens had to lay eggs colored and in baskets. Off they went Southwest to the little Churches where the ushers were cleaning the church hoping the Easter bunny would make it. They turned North to stop at the Langston Hughes Community Center and a quick stop at The Apollo for the community kids. The wind was picking up, so they're going as fast as Rudolph could. The August Wilson then Frederick Douglass Theatre then several stops on the coast. Rudolph was smiling: "I think we're going to make it!" But Bobby realized as they were about to cross Maine that he had one more basket. "My goodness!" Bobby declared. "We haven't delivered Ashley Bryan's basket. All the children will hate me if I don't get this to Mr. Bryan." Rudolph, like everybody, loved Ashley the best. They all would do anything to let Ashley know that. After all, look what Ashley has given to them. "We've got to turn around," Rudolph said. Mrs. Claus said, "Ashley will understand with this storm and all." But Rudolph and Bobby both said, "Yeah. But we won't. We have to turn around." Rudolph climbed telling Bobby and Sarah to hold on. Up he went to get on top of the storm. Then he made a sharp Left to swing back. "Bobby, do you know where Ashley lives?" "Of course I do." "Then you know I can't land. I'll get as low as I can, jump out. Sarah, keep the basket until EB's on the ground then let it go. EB, come to the pier as quickly as you can. I'm going to go around the island." But Bobby was worried about the wind and the ice. "If I'm not there you go on. I'll make it home." But Rudolph had seen the wolves and knew better. "Sarah, wrap up, this is going to be a bumpy ride."

Bobby jumped out near Langston Hughes Lane and Sarah let the basket go. EB caught it, putting it quickly on the front porch. Then as fast as he could hop started toward the pier. Rudolph got low and lower. They saw Bobby running and got as slow as they could. Sarah threw the blanket to Bobby. "Hang on, Bobby. We got you." She was a farm girl and much stronger than she looked. Rudolph knew he had to climb. "Got him!" Sarah said, and Ruddy pumped to get above the storm. The sky showed a streak of blue. They were going to make it.

"I'll drop you at the oak tree," Rudolph said. "You'll be safe from there." And he came as close to the ground as he dared and EB jumped out. He hippity hopped home. Standing at the door was Edna. Then he smelled it. Turnip soup with garlic! His favorite! "Where did you get the garlic?" he asked. "The Puffins were on their way home and saw you with Rudolph and thought you might need some good fresh garlic. Now tell me all about your trip."

Just as dawn was breaking Rudolph landed at the North Pole. David was waiting at one door and Santa at another. David said, "I'll walk Sarah home. Be right back." Santa was on crutches but Sarah could smell the bacon and knew a big bowl of grits and a pot of coffee was waiting. "I followed you on radar. You did a great job!" Santa said as he hugged her.

And David walked back to the barn to help put the sleigh away. As they walked into their home Rudolph smelled the hay sauteing. And he recognized the truffles browning with them. A glass of champagne was waiting. "You saved Easter," David said. "So you deserve the best." And they smiled.

And all three riders slept on happy dreams of a good job.

THE TRAIN RIDE

Her sister had left yesterday for Art Camp so though she wasn't lonely she was alone. The best part of that is she would have Mommy all to herself. Maybe Mommy would tell her a story or even maybe they could sing a song together. She never did learn how to harmonize and this would be a good time to learn. She set the table for the two of them. She had already dusted which was her usual job and she checked the basement door to be sure it was locked.

She had learned to slice ham from being with Grandmother last summer. She hadn't learned how to make biscuits and as it turned out she never would but she peeled tomatoes for a pretty salad and had gone to the backyard to pick fresh flowers for the table.

Mommy usually got home at 5:30 so everything would be ready. The greens were in the pot and would be heated as soon as Mommy came through the door. She pulled out her favorite book to wait.

Mommy came in smiling at her. "What a beautiful table," she exclaimed. "You're getting to be quite a little lady." Mommy gave her a hug. "I'm going to take a nap if you don't mind eating by yourself. You can turn on the TV; it won't bother me." And she said No. It's all right. Mommy went to bed and she ate her dinner. Alone.

She washed her dishes and set the table again for her father. He would be home about ten. She went into the bedroom she shared with her big sister and began packing her suitcase.

The suitcase was beautiful to her. It was a Lady Baltimore given to her by her godmother for her birthday. They were very different, she and her sister. She didn't want much and her sister wanted everything. She pulled her two dresses from the closet and her patent leather shoes for church. Her favorite sox were the pink ones with lace tops because she would want to look nice. Pajamas, underwear, and her five T-shirts. She only had three pairs of shorts because every time her mother asked if she wanted new ones she said No. She almost forgot her favorite books: *Mother West Wind* and *Mother West Wind's Children*. Now she was ready. Her blue jeans, T-shirt, and pink sweater were laid out. Tennis shoes and sox. She stretched out watching the moon play with the stars. And drifted off to sleep.

Mother always got up first. You could hear her brush her teeth, wash up, then off to the kitchen to make breakfast. She heard Father run the water to shave. She needed the bathroom but was determined to wait. Mommy was saying "I have to help pack." But she heard Father "I have to get to work on time; she knows how to put some clothes in a suitcase. I need to get started." Mommy came to peek. "Honey, get up. I have to go to work. Mr. Gray will be here at 9:30. Love you." But she pretended to be asleep. When she heard the car pull out of the driveway she rushed to the bathroom. Whew! She just made it.

MY FIRST VISIT WITH ASHLEY

The first time I visited Ashley I was as nervous as can be. I had taken the train up from Washington, DC, to Maine (change in Boston) for Portland. Then I had to find a way to the Pier to go to Islesford on the mail boat. It was a bumpy trip but we made it though wet, and since I'm a poor traveler, scared. There he stood waiting for me as if this was the greatest thing he had to do all day. A big hug and a fuss at because I hadn't told the mail boat I was coming to see him. He bought a ticket on the yearly basis and all you had to do was say you were with him. I actually thought he was worth the twenty dollars or so and we laughed. Up to his house where he lent me a dry shirt and dry sox. He then showed me around his marvelous home with all the toys, drawings, sketches and everything. I was most fascinated by the airplane line which you pulled and a plane flew from one side of the living room to the other. There was something childlike but also something sophisticated about the house. He ate early so we went out to dinner. I noticed he didn't lock the door. If they want to get in they'll find a way, he said. And being a nervous person I wondered how I would sleep.

Like a top. The quilt was warm, the stained glass beautiful and what the heck: if they wanted to get in they would. But they didn't.

I wanted to get up the next morning to walk the beach with him to see what had brushed up on shore but he was already gone. Then I understood: an artist must have some time alone. Like Gwen Brooks, Ashley did not do dishes so I washed and dried the dishes from who knows how long ago and settled down in his home. He came in empty-handed that day and we just talked or rather I listened to him talk about his life. I still don't know why he chose me to work with and to share. I kept urging him to do a book on his WWII days but he kept moving around the subject.

I was fortunate that he wanted to do a book with me. And I couldn't say Yes quickly enough. Like many who knew him and many who saw and admired his work I love him. I know you are not dead until you are forgotten and Ashley will never be dead.

LITTLE BROTHER/BIG BROTHER

(For Morris and David)

Little brothers look up
To Big Brothers
They share everything

Little brothers wear
Big brothers' left over
Blue jeans White shirts and
Their favorite tie
For Sunday school
And as they grow
Into them
Leather shoes that
Can be shined and shined
For Sunday school then
Recital of poems
Dances at the gym and on
Their first real date

Little brothers want
The same big brother friends
To play really well at
The same sports
And listen
To father and mother fight
On Saturday nights

Big brothers wish
They could be rich
And famous
And take care
Of everyone

They want
All things to be
Better

Little brothers and Big brothers
Visited this world
From an angel
Called Mom
And now
One gets to go
Home again

MATING TIME

(For a Lonely Meteorite Looking for Love)

Mating time
In the Galaxy

Sends messages
Whirling twirling
Dancing
Through Space

They come to
Third planet
From the yellow sun

But we are committed
To Blue

There may be a fight
Or maybe a flight
Or maybe a hug

Shaking us up

Love shouldn't frighten
Us

No means No

Go away Suitor

We are spoken
For

SOME COMPLAIN

Dear Anthonye Earle "Tonye" Perkins:

Thank you for inviting me to share good wishes. I do not email and have asked a friend to send this along to you. I'm sorry I cannot at this time take on the responsibility of a foreword, but as an ancestor I want to send some good wishes.

Some complain
When the wind blows strong
When the snow falls
Light
When the cloud grays up
But we never know
How important changes
Are
To giving the soil the strength
To produce new plants

Some of us should know
The sun will warm
The earth
And blossoms will
Come
How fortunate I am
To be a part of that weather
Thank you Anthonye for inviting me
To help introduce your energy and love
To another generation

WHEN WATER COULD NOT ENCOURAGE YOU

Congratulations to all of you who entered this essay competition. Special best wishes to those whose work was chosen to win but a sweet hug and a big hand clap to those who competed. Life is always about doing our best which sometimes is better than others and sometimes is simply our best. There is pride each time we walk out onto the court.

As a poet all I have are words. I think words are the most powerful weapons on Earth because words battle ignorance. Ignorance is worse than illness. With illness we may rest and get well, with ignorance we are only cruel. I should also add that with illness we get to stay in bed, eat hot soup and read books. Books are our best friends.

We are living in troubled times because there are those who would like to make us fearful. We are not afraid because we have words to give us dreams which make us strong.

I am so proud of all of you. You learned to walk though you tumbled a lot; you learned to swim though the water could not encourage you; you learned to have the training wheels taken off your bikes so that you could ride on your own dreams. Keep riding. Understand you will learn to fly. You will find the words that give you a beautiful song. Sing it. No one else has to hear it. It is yours. Sing on.

FOR THE 2023 GRADUATES OF ROANOKE COLLEGE

Congratulations!

No matter what our dreams or situations Words are the most
important evolution of human beings.
We speak, sing, write, pray in words.
We understand our pets and parents through words.
Words paint our dreams; words embrace our emotions.
We use words to make a better world.
We create words to prepare ourselves for a new world.
We gaze at the stars to understand our galaxy.

We look in a mirror to understand ourselves

Our eyes mirror the love we have for each other. Our words
deliver the words showing respect for others.

Life is a good idea.
We find words, write essays, allow our vulnerabilities to flow.
We do our best life with our living words.
We go forward because words do not go back.

We build a pyramid of words with our memories and sit in the sun
And be proud.

ANSWERS

What did you like about growing up in Cincinnati?

That's a hard question since I don't have anything to compare it with. Like I actually only grew up once and that was in Cincinnati. I guess you could say it made me love Skyline three ways and I used to love Graeters but they quit making Peach Sorbet in summer so I don't do them anymore. And we do have one of the great zoos which I loved and still love to visit but once when my school class went I was somehow lost and I had to figure out how to get home. The zoo folk got a policeman to put me on the 75 Bus for free. It couldn't happen now because everyone has a cell phone.

What was it like growing up Black?

The Black American experience in all America has been a beacon. We made American food unique and special; we made patches of cloth into quilts; we remind all of us of the importance of integrity and probably, to me, we are a forgiving group. We were taught that in church by our grandmothers. What would the American not only regional situations be without us?

Why do you think women want to work?

I think most women that I know work because they have children to feed; mothers and fathers to care for; husbands to supplement. Mostly.

What are you most proud of?

I am very proud that I am sane and for the most part happy.

Is there anything you'd like to say to Cincinnati?

Cincinnati is home and I am pleased to have been invited to share this wonderful event.

If you were running for president, what would be your campaign promises?

If I were running for president I would promise the nation I would create a Secretary of Athletics and we could then take a look at whether or not the athletes and the fans were being fairly treated.

INTRODUCING KNOXVILLE

(For Bill Walsh and Reinhardt University)

I am sharing "Knoxville, Tennessee," which is not only one of my favorite poems but a rather clear one. I was the first person in the Giovanni family to be born in a hospital: Knoxville General Hospital. I was, of course, born during the age of segregation so Knoxville General could just have easily been named Knoxville Colored. I had an older sister who was born at home. Home would have been my, or rather our, Grandmother's home. Grandmother and I'm sure a friend or someone who was a nurse helped bring my sister into the world. We forget the navel cord had to be cut and mother had to be sewn. We also forget how many women died in childbirth though there is no record at all of how many men created those pregnancies. Mommy was well taken care of and ultimately had her second daughter: me. I am three years younger than my sister.

During the age of segregation jobs were scarce. Though both my parents were graduates of Knoxville College, finding a job paying enough to take care of his family was not easy. My father had a friend in Cincinnati who told him about a job opening at Glenview School, which was a home for boys. They waited until my birth in June then moved to Cincinnati that September. I have a photograph of my sister and me standing on the steps of Glenview School. And there is a sort of memory of it but I'm not sure that I remember or just heard about it. My parents had difficulties, mostly I would imagine financially, and we moved to Woodlawn which was a village just outside, but now inside, Cincinnati.

What I remember about Woodlawn was the outhouse. Most people don't know outhouses now but ours was brown wood. I think I liked something about it because I felt safe there. My parents argued a lot and I could not hear the back-and-forth sitting in the outhouse. There were flowers there and I remember a clean smell. And I seem to always have seen a rabbit or maybe that was a dream.

After a while we moved to Wyoming, which is also a village, now a part of Cincinnati. We lived across from Aunt Lil and Uncle Rich which is where I had my first job. I would wash their breakfast dishes for a quarter a week. I don't know why Aunt Lil asked me to do that but she did. They only had coffee cups and glasses of orange juice. My sister who didn't really like to play with me would always come around on Saturday, when I got paid, to help me spend. I was old before I realized maybe that wasn't the right thing for her to do.

Then we bought a house in Lincoln Heights where my sister and I shared a room. I liked to dust, I still do, so that was my Monday job. Gary Ann was talented so she practiced her piano lessons, her dance lessons and her singing. I just like to dust.
Our parents still argued and it went to fighting. It became more than I could understand. It was always comforting to know summer was coming and Grandmother would send Reverend Abrums to the train station to pick us up.

I wrote a poem "Nikki-Rosa" because I knew I needed to make decisions about my life. I said I was happy because I recognized happiness is a decision. It was my first important poem. But "Knoxville, Tennessee" is always special to my heart because I had Grandmother to keep me warm.

I don't know why people write what they do or how they remember things. I just know it's your decision when you want to share and when you are not ready. It's your life. And you can't let anyone take it away from you.

“KNOXVILLE, TENNESSEE”

I always like summer
best
you can eat fresh corn
from daddy’s garden
and okra
and greens
and cabbage
and lots of
barbecue
and buttermilk
and homemade ice-cream
at the church picnic
and listen to
gospel music
outside
at the church
homecoming
and go to the mountains with
your grandmother
and go barefooted
and be warm
all the time
not only when you go to bed
and sleep

A BLUES FOR MOTHER

somebody heard my mother cry
she was standing in the middle of the road
somebody heard
my mother cry
standing in the middle of the road

she was watching my grandmother
transition
on her way to heaven
she was sad to see grandmother go
all the way to heaven

two sisters came
with two duck eggs
sorry to miss their friend
one was blind leading
the other sad
to see her go

in a field
with sun and rain
another friend would blossom
somewhere in another field
another friend would grow

and mommy stands there
in the middle of the road
wondering which way to travel

somebody heard my mother cry
standing in the middle of the road

another friend came blooming up
and that's how things should go

happy birthday to all who are born
and tears for those who leave
happy birthday to all who are born
and tears for all who leave

A FRIENDSHIP

(Re: Breaking Rules)

Growing up in a small town is both good and bad. Good because you learn to work the crowd, play the game, skip-to-my-lou as it were. You learn that people lie and their lies don't matter. You also learn folk tell the truth but truth doesn't change anything. And if you're attentive you learn that the only things that matter are who loves you . . . and who doesn't. Not why you are loved nor did you deserve it but only that you are loved.

We grew up in a small town, Knoxville, Tennessee. Frankie was the leader of the group. This is what I first remember. I was sitting in the Gem Theatre getting ready to see a movie I have already forgotten. Frankie and five or six other girls came in. They sat behind me. Frankie recognized me. She said to another girl, "That's Nikki, Ms. Watson's granddaughter. Should we ask her to sit with us?" Everybody said some form of "yeah" or "ok" and they asked me if I wanted to sit with them. I didn't.

What I remembered is that Frankie and I went way further back than that. Our mothers were both members of Delta Sigma Theta. Our fathers both chased the dreams men chase when they marry the women of their dreams. Frankie was a privileged black American. She had the house, the car, the money, the church named after her family. I was in Knoxville because my parents fought and I couldn't make any sense out of it. I was hoping my grandmother would let me live with her and if she said "No" I didn't know what I was going to do. No. I did not want to sit with Frankie and her friends in a segregated movie house. I wanted to find a way out of my nightmare.

Grandmother understood way more than I thought and I enrolled in school. There are photographs of Frankie and me at her Aunt Helen's. We are cigarette girls. We have on pink little tutu dresses. I guess you call them tutus. We looked sweet. In those days, when people still smoked, the host and hostess would buy a carton of cigarettes and open them. Frankie and I would walk through the grounds at the lawn parties or the house when it was winter, offering cigarettes to the guests. It was a pretty cool thing to do. Grandmother and I would walk from Mulvaney Street to Dandridge Pike. She couldn't drive and I was too young. We didn't have a car either though I must point out we did almost have a car. A Plymouth, black, two door. The salesman drove it to our door. But Grandmother never could learn to drive and I was too young. The salesman came and took it back. Grandmother's money was returned. We walked.

And I would put on my costume. I suppose I loved it but I don't remember it that well. It was pink. And there were things, like little tiaras, on our heads. We looked cute. Helen was a fun person. The reason I make a great martini to this day is Helen Lennon would let me, or, I suppose, teach me, to make an extra dry. My Grandmother had a cousin named Diecennia who was married to an undertaker, Calvin Hardwick. Diecennia and Calvin had a fabulous home. Closets within closets to hold furs and jewelry and stuff. I spent part of a summer with them once. Diecennia also liked martinis. Stirred not shaken. She would take her soak and call for her martini. I learned to utilize my knowledge to produce a perfect martini. Diecennia and Calvin also had a slot machine. Calvin would give me quarters and I would try to win. I never did. And it wasn't until I took a voyage on the *QEII* that I understood it is not a gamble: the house will win; and you will lose. I haven't pulled a slot since. Calvin died first. My aunt Agnes and I went to Chattanooga to visit Di. I don't remember much of the visit but I did ask about the slot machine. It had been sold. Di passed and I don't remember when nor where I was. The martini stayed.

I wish I had understood I was not the only person in pain during those teenage years. I wish I had understood I was not the only person looking for someone to love. I got lucky. My mother's friends reached out; my teachers, Miss Delaney and Mme. Stokes, reached out; and most especially the librarian, Miss Brooks, reached out and I somehow held on. I went one morning to the Bijou theatre to see *Gog*, which was not all that good a movie but I had walked up to the front to get my ticket. I was, of course, sent to the back where I climbed the steps to watch Richard Egan in a science fiction show. It wasn't so much the back stairs as the sort of smirk on the ticket taker's face. That was my last movie for an awfully long time. Even now I prefer to buy them than to go see them. Joe Mack and I went to UT to see the live performance of the musical *L'il Abner* and we sat in the balcony but I don't know why.

Frankie and the gang went to camp and Grandmother sent me to camp with them. They put a frog in my bed which everybody laughed at but me. The frog was smothered by me and I did not like killing it. Had I known I would have stripped the bed. Everybody could swim but me. I still can't swim. And the idea that camp was supposed to be fun still escapes me. I almost got kicked out but having been already kicked out of the Brownies, camp was minor. I made it through camp but that was the last thing. I was kicked out of college; fired from my first job; just generally misunderstood so quite naturally I became a writer.

Frankie had written *Julie and the Beatniks*, which was produced in high school. Forty years later I learned that I was Julie. I was the rebel. I never thought of myself like that. I was, to me, the girl who didn't make cheerleading squad though I tried out. I was the girl who couldn't fast dance. I was the girl who watched. I was the girl outside.

Frankie's play *Breaking the Rules* should be subtitled *Growing Up Black and Privileged*. Frankie has a story to tell. She negotiated a very narrow path; she walked the line. Every generation has its Zora Neale Hurston, its voice of truth and clarity. Frankie Lennon is finding her way to a generational truth. It is not always a happy or funny story. But it is another side of a fabulous generation that changed the world. We all should be *Breaking the Rules*. We all need to read Frankie Lennon.

TOMORROW

I wish I was a star
Not the kind on stage
Where crowds and crowds
Shouted and clapped
And every time I looked around
I had another photo shoot
Or interview or somebody wanted me
To do something important . . .
But the kind floating
Quietly around the sky
Twinkling at the beautiful blue Earth
Or smiling at my cousins on Mars
And when I had the time
Going up to Jupiter and playing with my friends
on one of the Merry-Go-Round strings

Or maybe I'd like to be
A shark swimming
In the middle of the ocean learning
From my big brother just because
The water is warmer it is not
Safer to go too close
To the shore
Humans are not good friends

Perhaps most of all I think
I'd like to be a bat
Resting in the caves with my family
My mother teaching me to fly
Without wings
Just to trust her embrace
As we take off at midnight
Some would say we are ugly but mother
Would kiss me

And tell me she loves me
And I am the most wonderful daughter
She ever has had

But mostly I think
If I had just one wish
I would wish
uncle ernie would
STOP

HER DREAMS

Mommy always wanted
To be famous

She would have us (my sister and me)
Sing
In all the talent shows
But I could not carry the harmony
Then she had me
Sing
Alone
Though The Isley Brothers
Always won
Ronald's sweet voice and Vernon
Doing "the Itch"
Sort of like Michael Jackson
Doing "the Moon Walk"
So I and all others
Lost

We sang
In harmony
On our front desk
September In The Rain
And our neighbors loved it
Especially Mrs. Morris who
Covered lightly with a quilt
Clapped after each song

Then while waiting
For the Number 16 Bus
She would say:
"This Is June/Hold your tune"
And we had to sing
My Blue Heaven

"but Mommy" . . . my sister would say . . .
"No is out here"

Maybe someone will come by
And hear us
So we sang
Until the bus arrived

She and my sister sat
Together

I sat on the other side
Alone

ALTARS

Grandpapa, John Brown Watson, they called him "Book," graduated Fisk University in 1905 and married a Spelman girl. I wish he had known Ashley Bryan. Grandpapa liked to read. Ashley liked to draw. Grandpapa was from Albany, Georgia. Ashley from the North. Both were quiet men who loved art. Grandpapa majored in Latin. After graduation the family had to decide what to do with Grandpapa so they decided he should teach. In those days teaching was a political job and the Watsons were well connected despite segregation and other southern problems. Grandmother, Emma Louvenia, graduated Albany Normal School. She was a very pretty woman which helped smooth her road. They saw each other at school meetings and occasionally he walked her home. Though she had a political job she spoke up in meetings. She became a "race woman" demanding her rights. Anything Grandpapa needed or wanted was taken care of around the dinner table. His wife was a pretty woman with what was called ladylike manners. Everybody liked her. But Grandpapa with his Latin and Greek stories, with his St. James Bible, with the Spirituals that he loved so much became enchanted with Grandmother. Soon it was evident there was a family problem. Grandpapa wanted Grandmother which caused more than a voice raising at the dinner table and the family took what was essentially a "vote." It didn't matter. Grandpapa was in love. He wanted and got a divorce and asked Grandmother to marry him. When I went to live with them in Knoxville, Tennessee, many many years later my job was to wash dishes. Grandpapa would keep me company while Grandmother went to the porch to have a cigarette after cooking dinner. "You know, Nikki," he would say, "I only wanted to kiss your grandmother." He was smiling. And no matter where she was in the house or on the porch she would call back, "John Brown, if I had let you kiss me you would have never married me." It took me years before I understood that was a metaphor. Maybe that was the beginning of my writing career but I'm a bit ahead of myself.

They married and the family purchased a small home for them. Grandmother always loved flowers and her front garden was beautiful. One day a white woman was driving by or I should say was driven by and she saw Grandmother's flowers. Her driver stopped and called Grandmother over to the car. The white woman wanted to know how much Grandmother wanted for her flowers. Grandmother's response was she didn't grow flowers to sell. Grandmother had a tone. When Grandpapa came home from school she told him about it. He knew immediately there was a problem. He went to see his father and brothers. They knew a problem was coming. Grandpapa's father went to the white woman's husband to apologize and see how the situation could be resolved. That evening the woman's husband came in his buggy to get an apology from Grandmother. Grandmother was not in the mood. "I don't grow flowers," Grandmother repeated, "for anybody but my family." As far as she was concerned that was that. The man said to Grandpapa, "We can solve this if I can give her five lashes." Grandpapa we must remember was in love so that was out. The man told the horse to Giddy up and everybody knew what would happen that night. The Watsons are gun people and they all gathered at Grandpapa's. The other wives and children were taken to The Watson Building where goods were bought and sold. One of the brothers stayed with them with the instruction to kill anything that came toward the building. The Watson Building still stands in Albany. While they waited they had a family discussion. John Brown, they declared, this woman has caused us our reputation and maybe our lives. We think, I think, you need to move along. There is a teaching job in Knoxville and I hear the Presbyterians are opening a college. I'm going to get a letter off to see if you can't get one of the jobs. They sat and waited. When the klan came his father walked out to the man in front. "My daughter-in-law is sick. We are sending her off to get better. She didn't know what she was doing. We are very sorry if there was any hurt." The woman's husband knew what he was seeing. Someone would get killed and most likely it would be him. "We know you and we know you are sorry. Come on, boys.

Let's go home." And they packed up Grandmother and Grandpapa the next day and sent them to Knoxville. Where I was the first person in the family to be born in the old Knoxville General Hospital. My sister used to tease me saying they picked up the wrong baby but I think I'm a Watson.

I went to Fisk University as an Early Entrant. I had, I have, my Grandmother's temperament though it took me some while to understand it. I was kicked out of Fisk for disobeying the rules. I was wrong and luckily when I reapplied Blanche Cowan was Dean. And Walter Leonard was President. My Fisk family was complete. Grandpapa transitioned before I graduated. One of the reasons I was kicked out was I left campus without permission. I went back to Knoxville to have Thanksgiving Dinner with my grandparents. It was the right thing to do but I still was wrong. No matter.

John Lewis and Diane Nash left our campus to join the Civil Rights Movement forming SNCC. John and I graduated at the same time but for different reasons: He left to give life to the Constitution of the United States; I for disobeying silly rules.

I'm sorry we have not made the major change we could make. At our beginning we went against the grain and become a co-ed college. I'd like to see us go against the grain and become a woman's university. I'd like to see us have a women's tennis team that is international; a women's golf team; a culinary school of international standing. And while we will always keep and need and want our Jubilee Singers, we can borrow some men from Vanderbilt, Tennessee State, even Meharry if they have time and certainly Belmont University. We need a tour of our singers just as the big rich schools tour their athletes. We need to change. John and Diane helped make a change that W. E. B. Du Bois started. Fisk had Robert Hayden and Aaron Douglas. We need a change from a segregated world to a nonsegregated world while recognizing racism is still with us. We need to understand if we want an integrated world we will have to integrate. We need to understand freedom isn't free. Each generation pays a price. Ashley Bryan went to WWII and crawled on his belly while bullets flew overhead to draw the story of Black Soldiers. I'm glad I'm a Fiskite who recognizes we all are "Ever On The Altar."

HOME

(For Beauford Delaney)

It's lonely being genius
Not being understood
Never throwing the football
Or racing the other kids
Not being interested
In picking on the smaller kids
Hating the way other kids
Teased
And made cry
Those who needed a friend

Enough to make you
Run away from Home

But Home is never run from
Home is always in our hearts and certainly in
Our memories
We paint Home
Even though it does not look like
Home
And off we go to France
To make friends
With famous geniuses
Even though we miss Home
And even though no one recognizes
We are lonely

Art makes you lonely
Because
Art wants
To be your only friend
Art wants all your love

So you try to wander back
Home

Your Art is understood to be great
But you are still lonely

Your greatness will come

Not now
Not any time soon
but in your heart which flies
Back Home
While your body rests
In another land at
Another time

Your Art
Embraces you
And those who have loved
You
Will keep your Art
    Alive

LETTER TO THE EDITOR

Letters to the Editor
The Roanoke Times
201 Campbell Ave. SW
Roanoke, VA 24011-1105

Dear Editor:

I write in gentle sadness to join the silent tears of the Class of Twenty-Twenty. Our students have worked so hard to be allowed to walk across that stage, shake a hand, have a photo made of that wonderful Hokie smile. Their parents of near and far have worn sweaters that their daughters could wear coats; worn down beat boots so that their sons could wear shoes but they have not put laughter aside; they have not put pride on the back burner. They have waited, many of them, for that day to see their child be the first, if not the only, to hold high a degree.

I join the Class of Twenty-Twenty in the hope that a monument will find a home on our campus engraved with their names. We have acknowledgment to our soldiers of war; we embrace the names of those lost in the tragedy. The Class of Twenty-Twenty having given up the joy of throwing their caps to the heavens shouting Go Hokies deserve no less.

We hope there will be room, for the love they have given us, on our campus by engraving their names on a monument so that one day when their children and grandchildren join the Hokie family they will know the Class of Twenty-Twenty when called upon made the necessary sacrifice also.

Ut Prosium,
Nikki Giovanni
University Distinguished Professor

GRADUATION POEM

I join----- in gentle sadness and silent tears the pride of the class of Twenty-Twenty in accepting their duty

I join----- the unheard steps across the stage
And the shouts when that diploma is put in their hands

I join----- the bravery of the class of Twenty-Twenty in understanding: some gave their health; some gave their lives; some gave their possibility of kindness because of the selfishness of others

I join----- the understanding of forgiveness

I join----- my students in writing about their first kiss and
I join----- them in the heartbreak when he is gone

I join----- the laughter after a winning football game
And the pouts when UVA finally almost evened the score

I join----- our parents who struggled to make a day possible that is not possible but that will always be possible because The Hokie Nation is the possibility

I join----- us all in the struggle to be a better nation through the betterment of ourselves

I join----- those who hope our campus will find room for a monument to celebrate these youngsters. Most of our monuments honor those who cannot know how we praise them.

I join----- those who praise the living

I join----- all of the Hokie family who welcome the newest Hokie members

Who one day will bring their grandchildren to show "See? I was a different soldier in a different war"
I join----- the pride we take in our Hokie family

The Class of Twenty-Twenty has been gracious and brave

I join----- all of us all over the globe who applaud their sacrifice

Congratulations Class of Twenty-Twenty and Twenty-Twenty-One

I join----- the sun shining for your warmth and the rain for quenching your thirst
Spring will come and winter will be embraced

I join----- all people of good will to wish you
Congratulations

A DEDICATION

It actually takes four people
To write a book:
The writer who writes it
The critic who talks about it
The librarian who stocks it
The teacher who teaches it
I thank the first one who has the courage
And I acknowledge the other three for their part
In watering this seed
And helping it grow

FALL IN LOVE

(For Artemis)

If you have to fall
In love

And you

It should be with a book

Not a novel
Nor a mystery
Certainly nothing scary
And always remember other life forms
Aren't aliens but other life forms
Just as we are earthlings
Not people to be feared and killed
But life forms inhabiting the same planet

Maybe ideally a recipe anthology
With great ideas of things to do with garlic
Or especially a mixology book to tell us how to relax
If we are careful
We all need to know how to taste beer
And how to judge wine
(the same way we do people—carefully)

And we definitely need a book that lets us
Laugh
And every now and then one
That lets us cry

We need a book and a dog
And a quilt
To tuck into

And love
That will be faithful
And true

That's what love is:
A good book

1038 BURNS

Our home was like a railroad track
Or maybe a rocket
The kitchen
Then their bedroom
The bathroom
The stairs leading outside
And my bedroom that I shared
With my big sister

Mommy didn't have a job
So she waited up
For my father who had two

I waited up
For her

She sang Time After Time
Dreaming out the window
And I dreamed out too looking
For Mars
The Red planet would go by and I thought:
There is something wrong
The Red planet had to have water
So it could grow tomatoes and lettuce
What would make it rain

A Library would help answer
It had to be that there was a global war and Mars blew up
And burned
And burned
Until there was nothing
And no one

Like my home on Saturday night
When my parents argued

I only wanted to tilt our apartment
And take off to the galaxy
But my godmother would come to remind us
My sister and me
That it was all going to be all right

Mommy got a job
And we bought a house
That reminded me of the Titanic
And I wanted it
To drown
But instead I was lucky
and went to live
with my grandparents
and learned something
about love
    I dusted and cleaned the pantry
And helped peel the veggies
And made myself useful
Waiting for the Red planet
To cool down

Because I knew
If any earthling was needed
In Space it was a Black Woman
Since we had lived
With aliens all our lives
We could continue

Mars is our sister
We are not afraid
We are Black women
We travel forth

400 MULVANEY STREET

It was a small house
In a small neighborhood
Their bedroom was in the front overlooking the front porch
Mine in the back sharing a window
Into our next-door neighbor's home
Edith White always closed the curtains
When darkness arrived

The living room held a piano
Which I never learned to play
And a television set that I remember
Being awakened
To see Lena Horne on
Ed Sullivan
The couch was a rose color print and I still have it
Though now it holds mostly my books
And a quilt given to me when I was diagnosed
With lung cancer

Our kitchen held a pantry
That I arranged
And waxed
Until the mice gave up
And went away

Grandpapa purchased Grandmother
A stove that had a deep well
A forerunner to the Slow Cooker

The refrigerator never held chicken eggs
They lay in a triangular dish
Which I still have with blue pink
And dark brown eggs

We had a back porch
That had a rollaway bed for anyone
Passing through
Who needed a place to rest

The dining room was special and precious
The dining room table was covered with white lace
And always fresh flowers
In the corner was a cake platter with a crystal top
And in the cabinet were the Sunday dishes
That we used only when we had company

There was a drawer holding
Her sterling silver that she had purchased one
Setting at a time
I polished regularly just in case
The Book Club or Civil Rights Women
Or even the Church women would come by
To have Tea and discuss their next move
Against segregation

I was in college when I got a ride
Home to spend a surprise
Thanksgiving with them

I arrived on Wednesday and was so glad to be
Home
It was obvious Grandmother had not planned
Anything special but now I was
Company

She scooted across the alley to get a chicken
From Reverend Abrams
And my job became stringing the beans

She was up early Thursday to wring
The neck and I had to pluck the feathers

We stuffed it with cornbread
Put the green beans on with a strick of lean
Grandpapa and I both loved bread pudding
And luckily she had some stale bread
No ice cream today but a wonderful salad
That I still don't know
How she put together

The bathroom was between the two bedrooms and as I heard
The water running I knew
Everyone had to bathe
Grandmother first with her beloved Sweetheart Soap
Then she helped Grandpapa
He put his favorite tie on
And I noticed he was moving a bit slower but I thought
It was all right

I bathed in the tub with fresh water and tried to look
Dressed up
That evening as we three sat at the table
Grandpapa said the blessing
And I lied about how well I was doing
In college

My ride back to Nashville came
That night and I kissed them both
Never knowing
That would be our Last Thanksgiving

He went to Heaven three months later
I have never bathed since

I received a call: call your Grandmother
And the only telephone number I remember even now
Is 3-1593.
I knew when I dialed he was gone
And all that I knew of love
Would also be buried

BAY LEAVES

I watched Mommy
Cook
Though I cooked
With Grandmother

With Grandmother I learned
To pluck chickens
Peel carrots
Turn chittlins inside out
Scrub pig feet

With Mommy I watched
Leftovers for stew
Or vegetable soup
Great northern beans
Mixed collards turnips and mustard greens
Garlic cloves Bay Leaves
Very beautifully green
Stiff . . . so fresh
With just a pinch of salt
Not everything together
All the time but all the time
Keeping everything

I make my own
Frontier soup in a crock pot
I make my own ice cream with a pinch of salt
And everything else
With garlic
But fresh Bay Leaves
Are only for very special
Ox Tails

EDNA LEWIS

After Hours in the Watershed

Some call it history; some gossip. There is always something if not being hidden then not being discussed. The abdication of the British king was a powerful thing so let's call it love. He loved a twice divorced woman whom he could not marry so off they go for her to nestle with the nazis and him to . . . what? A part of him loved the American music the Black folk were creating. That's what Paris was for. And there was Bricktop who owned three cafés and needed someone to cook for the jazz players. As Paris fell Bricktop took her cook from Nevis and her American jazz into Spain. For a promise of return to his crown and a title for his wife (though some point out Wallis was spying for the nazis) Edward visited the nazis and Bricktop knew it was time to cross the ocean back to her home. She took Edna Lewis with her. The girl from the Caribbean brought her beauty, her charm and her spices. And became her own type of queen. Bricktop mentored the British singer Mabel Mercer who mentored Bobby Short, and the Harlem Renaissance moved downtown. The former king and his wife could sit and smoke marijuana (which is now legal), watch the dancing and be safe until the war was over. The nazi past was a secret; the love of jazz moved on. And the food Edna created was passed on to Scott Peacock and cookbooks. The beauty delighted the palate as well as the eye. And I have a photo in my automobile of Edna and me when she came to visit in Virginia. I still don't know how to make biscuits and I never could sing but I'm happy to remind history that maybe he loved Wallis or not: it was the music and the food that he needed to be near.

DETROIT

They heard the motors
And packed up their families

Going north

From:
Alabama Georgia Mississippi
Both Carolinas
Sharecropping
Being cheated
Being cursed
Not able to vote
Being scared
Sometimes being lynched
(Just for the fun of it)

They headed north
To Detroit
Fixing motors
Tightening wheels
Renting decent apartments
Sending their kids to school

They headed north
Taking their talent for the guitar
Beating a proper beat on a drum
Blowing a trumpet
Playing piano in church and outside too
(with just a little sass)

Singing the old rhythms
With new lyrics
Winding their children up
Like little dolls to sing

On street corners
In talent shows
Anywhere they could be heard
So the family could become
Millionaires
Or drug addicts
They encouraged
Writing poems

Publishing little books
Going to festivals
All those things
That encourage

They opened little eat shops
With the best oxtails
Navy beans
And Lordy what they could do
With a fried chicken

Everybody went to Mattie's
"Early in the morning"

And Detroit became
The Voice of Young Black America
That the world copied

AN ANGEL LIKE ASHLEY

What does a poem
Look like
Well of course you can read
The words
Or admire the paper
And even wonder why
This metaphor embraced
That simile
But to see a poem
You need
An angel

You may wonder
What a poem tastes like
Yes you can swirl
The batter
Add sugar
An egg (well beaten)
And bake
But to taste a poem
You need an angel

Sometimes you're cold
Or sad
Or lonely
And you need something
Or someone to comfort
You
And you turn
To a poem
Because an angel
Comes to rub your back

How does a poem
Sound
Like an angel
Blowing a saxophone
Or a vibraharp
Or most likely like Ashley Bryan
Reading to us
From Heaven

JANUARY 26, 2020

(The Death of Kobe Bryant)

We don't know
She does
He did
I can't
You don't
Know the last words
"The weather is bad
Don't go
Stay home
They will be all
Right with out
You"

We don't know
And actually it's not
Our business
Was she worried
Did she feel something
Did she wish
He would for once
Listen

But she most likely kissed
Them both wondering
What they might want
For dinner
Or snacks into the evening
When they came home

She hoped they would
Win
But she was so tired

Maybe just a short
Nap
Just to close
Her eyes
For a minute
She was cold
Just needed to throw
A blanket over
Her feet
For just a minute

We don't
Know what
She thought
Or said

It's none
Of our business
And too sad
To think
about

ANNOUNCING SPRING

(Happy Birthday Emma Joahanne Thomas-Smith)

The wind dances
Across the Prairie
Bringing a song
Of hope
And prayer
Clearing a way for
Emancipated souls
To communicate
And learn

They lay their bodies
Under the grasslands
That the Crocuses
Will grow
And Emma will smile
Bringing the sun
Announcing
Spring

AVEC VOUS

My Latin is limited
My Greek is worse
And the languages
And signs
The drawings
The bones
We find

Some neatly buried
Some spread Apart
Perhaps by storm
Perhaps War
Maybe big animals
Looking for a meal
Maybe the ants
Or underground life forever
Looking for a home

Maybe just two lovers
Holding on
To each other
As the fire burns
Or rocks roll over
As planes fall
Or even water with all
Its force
Pushing mud
Or tree roots
Or something
But not the Love
That holds the two
Together

And they whisper
To each other

Don't wait for me
I'll be there

I'll see you
Soon

BETTY WILLS JACOBY SKINNER

7 April 1925–31 July 2020

Death is a natural part of life though we celebrate it differently from birth. Betty Skinner had the warmth of her youngest daughter, Virginia C. Fowler's hand, to hold as she transitioned. And the comfort of family members who preceded her.

As with many women Betty's age higher education was not a choice but she worked as hard as she could to see that Ginney, as she was called, attended and graduated from college. Betty was especially proud that Ginney earned her Ph.D. and would brag to all who would listen. Betty had a love of her family and collected all the knowledge about them that she could. She enjoyed sharing her stories with her six grandchildren and many nieces and nephews.

Betty and her second husband, Albert Skinner, moved to Blacksburg to be closer to and cared for by Ginney, her only surviving daughter. Her oldest daughter, Diana Roane, had passed, as had her brother Harlan and sister Charline Jacoby. Her younger sister, Georgianna Jacoby, is not well and lives in Waxahachie, Texas, with family.

There is the thought that death is the end but there can never be an end where love has been sown. The seeds of love have been carried by the birds and the wind and the rain to settle in the embrace of soil. Some seeds grow and some will turn and turn until they become stones of value to those who find them. Some are diamonds and some are rocks but all keep returning to the love that was put next to them as they began their rest. We are birthed with our mothers but we only have the comfort loneliness brings as she transitions.

A TOAST TO POEMS

We need a poem because
Sometimes
We are lonely

We need a poem because
We have sometimes lost our way

We need poems because
The dog is in the yard barking
At the neighbors and the soup
Is boiling over and we
Are thinking *I'm Sick*
Of Earth . . . I'm going Into Space
To Find another Life

We need poems because
They tell us we already
Have a wonderful life
Here

Let's raise our glasses
For how wonderful it
Is that poems take
Such good care
Of us

COMMENCEMENT DURING COVID

Many are saying how difficult this last year has been because of the pandemic but aside from the sadness of those we lost, we who are artists have found some comfort in ourselves. We have lived in a world too much concerned with what others think about us or are doing with their lives and this Covid has given us the time to think within our own hearts and minds. We have had time to read and reflect; we have had the courage to learn to cook our grandmother's fried chicken recipe and we took the time to cut Grandpapa's grass. We carried food to the hungry and clothes for the Suit Closet. We could not sing together in church but we could use our Zoom to sing with each other virtually. We contacted old friends and sometimes we allowed our essays to be shared.

Congratulations to all of you who reached out to help the world be warmer, calmer and a better place. When you get your driver's license don't forget to register to vote. Walk your dog. Hug your mom. Congratulations to all of you.

CRAFT

I have no craft. I only have language which I try to weave into— What? A something. I have a love of quilts. No matter the weather so I weave my words into something to make me warm or keep me dry. I love stews, any stew, so I keep whatever is left over to percolate all day. If I'm lucky I'll make biscuits to go with it. But I must confess: I cannot roll out my biscuits like my grandmother did. I can, however, make drop biscuits which I slather in butter and to be honest I drink cheap champagne so it's a meal. I think jazz is incredibly important and I have to snap my fingers and when I'm alone I do a little dance my mother called The Geek. Nat King Cole when he was still with his trio sang it but it's almost impossible to find now. My favorite way of teaching myself how to tell a story is by listening to The Spirituals. What does it mean "to pray"? We cross Jordan or we bathe in Jordan. We lean on the Everlasting Arms. I love the comfort but there is also a story. I try to bring out what I learn. John Lewis and Milt Jackson, Connie Kay and Percy Heath taught me a lot about royalty. I could listen to *Fontessa* over and over again though that is not craft; that is learning. The stars talk to us if we just will have enough sense to listen. We recognize the similarities between The Middle Passage and the Galaxy. We understand the necessity of Black Americans to lead the way to the next world. We know we will carry our okra pods and a peanut. We understand the need to create beer from peanuts. I can go on and on and on. But I lack the craft to show how that should be done. If I could double patience I would make okra whisky. I lack the craft to show how that would be done but I do make great fried chicken wings. Our ancestors hid treasures away in home cellars where they rested with coal in a song, in a dance, in a story or a look. I don't have a craft. I have a love of the people who traveled the ocean to become a new people. I don't have a craft. I have the embrace and trust of my ancestors. And the language we created.

A RECIPE FOR THE *NEW YORK TIMES*

(Sent to Elizabeth A. Harris)

Dear Liz: you caught me off guard with my recipe. I'm a southern cook so I use whatever is around. Cut the chicken up or if you are lucky and working purchase wings. There is no such thing as too much butter. A half stick is usually good, though. Put a couple of cloves of garlic in the skillet to let them simmer. I like to rub the wings with ginger but I forgot to tell you a shake or two of nutmeg really helps. If summer get your rosemary from the garden or your tarragon or whatever is green growing. Do not roll a lot of flour on them. Just enough to cover then shake off. Do not batter them. You are not, after all, a chef trying to stretch your money. You may ask what about salt. As a Black woman I can tell you if you walked into the doctor's office with the toes of a child hanging from your vagina the first thing he would say to you is: You eat too much salt. It would take you a few minutes to explain to him you are having a baby so I have learned to be very cautious about salt. Now here is what is important: Cook slowly. If you don't have time to slowly fry then remember the old blues song: Come back tomorrow and try it again. You can substitute cinnamon but I prefer nutmeg.

THE CHRISTMAS LETTER

Dear David:

I thought I should drop you a note that I sent to and received from Santa. I recognized I was grumpy when we talked and though I know neither words nor deeds can be undone or unsaid and I am not a big fan of forgiveness I thought nonetheless I should drop a note to Santa to see what he thought of me, it being so close to Christmas and all. I did not expect to hear back from him since he and the elves not to mention Mrs. Claus are so busy right now but I did want to share that I knew I was grumpy talking with you. Much to my surprise I heard back and he said Don't worry, You are still and always on my Nice List. That made me so happy. Knowing you reporters check everything I am sending this note to you because Santa's note may not have gotten to my file yet and I want to be sure you are up-to-date. I hope you had a happy thanks/giving which should also be understood as thanks/taking. I look forward to talking with you next week.

Poetically, Nikki

21 MAY 2020

This is a letter of sadness to the *New York Times*:

Recently Jericho Brown accepted the Pulitzer Prize for Poetry. We who read poetry, which not everyone does, but we who do, were, or rather are, so proud. We have watched Jericho grow confident in his voice and his vision. As one of the old ladies who has worked with many of the youngsters I was thrilled to learn of this acknowledgment of his work.

Throughout these years of laboring in the poetic vineyard I have been fortunate to have developed a "gang." Whenever one of us is creating a program the other two fall in. I called Kwame Alexander and Dr. Joanne Gabbin to say let's get a page in the *New York Times* to celebrate Jericho. They both immediately said Yes.

What none of us knew was the cost of a page. My heart sank when I understood. Everyone knows Poets don't really have what is called "money." We also know ugly things like if the three of us robbed a bank we would make the front page; or if a girl or something was missing we would have our photos on a page with vile and vicious things said about us. So my thought is why not let the three of us celebrate our younger brother and perhaps help some other youngster, male or female, gay or straight, know there is a community out here who cares about him or her? I remember someone, who will be unnamed, had a page in the *Times* calling for the execution of five innocent youngsters. I suppose that is business but isn't a part of our business to lift up the community. The *Times* means a lot to the newspaper world. It would mean a lot for us to congratulate Jericho. I can proudly share I have a good supply of both toilet paper and paper towels that I would gladly give to you since we are only talking about paper. Money is just paper, too, but I have less of green and more of white. I am, however, willing to make a trade.

I write without the knowledge of my gang who are probably embarrassed that I am essentially begging but some things are worth begging for. Genius is one of them. Won't you consider giving us a page of praise? Joanne is a critic and I can do everything to get her to review a book for you; Kwame is a wonderful writer and he can be persuaded to write a story. I know this is still less than the cost of your page but I do have quite a bit of white paper. I hope you will consider helping us smile.

Poetically,
Nikki Giovanni

FISK

A Song of Freedom

I met the Queen of England. Of course it is obvious that she called me, or perhaps more accurately, her people called my people to say she would like to meet me. The Queen is a horsewoman and she was coming to Richmond, Virginia, to see a horse and they wanted to know if I would mind coming to Richmond to meet her. Since she is the Queen and I'm not the easy answer was "Yes."

Richmond is only about a two-hour drive from Blacksburg and it was a pretty day.

I have to admit I didn't want to stand in one of those lines where she and Prince Philip walked down one side then another and said things like "How was your trip" and "Thank you for coming" but since I had committed through Virginia Tech, my university, I didn't want to embarrass them so I decided "Yes" I would stand in one of those lines. But that was not the case. When I arrived at the hotel I was taken to a special room where a reception was being held. Important people like our governor and senators were there. Some of whom I knew. Food and drink were being passed around but since I never drink with strangers I passed on the drink and pretended to enjoy the food.

Her people were taking her one way and Prince Philip's people were taking him the other. I was just sort of standing there not knowing what was expected of me when her gentleman brought the Queen over and introduced me. Since I knew who she was I was the one being introduced. She complimented me on my poetry and especially on the poem I had read after the tragedy at Tech.

I was surprised that she had followed our sadness or even that she might have known some of my poems. I actually still think her people tell her things as they escort her to the next person but it's still nice to think of the Queen of England piled up in bed, fire glowing, a glass of wonderful red wine on her nightstand, reading to Philip my love poems. I am a couple of inches taller than the Queen and there was something I wanted to say to her. Meeting famous people is difficult because you are nervous and they want to move on but I thought "when" will I ever have this opportunity again so I stepped in front of her. Not blocking her but just enough to keep her from turning away. Because I am a smidgen taller she had to look up. "We have something in common," I said to her. I wish I could find a way for you to catch her voice because that's so much of really telling what she was thinking: "Oh?" she said.

"I am a graduate of Fisk University in Nashville, Tennessee. Your great-grandmother, Queen Victoria, invited the Fisk Singers, through the good offices of her cousin Lord Nottingham, through the prayers of Reverend Stowe, the brother of Harriet Beecher Stowe, to come to England because he wanted Her Majesty to hear the Spirituals. The Fisk Singers were thrilled because they were singing to raise money to keep our college alive.

"The Nine Singers stayed in the castle with the Queen for over a year. Those young men and women, who had only recently been released from slavery, were required to interact with hereditary royalty. They had to conduct themselves as if they had always been free. In the evening they performed for the Queen and her guests. As you know during those times royalty did not talk to commoners but Her Majesty one evening leaned down from her throne to ask: 'Where are you from?' And Ella Shepard answered: 'Nashville, Your Majesty.' And the Queen responded: 'Why that must be a musical city.' And Nashville has been known as Music City from thenceforth.

"Queen Victoria had her portrait painter paint their portraits and she awarded them fifty thousand pounds which saved Fisk. I just thought you might like to know."

Queen Elizabeth looked up at me and said, "Oh. I did not know. Thank you."

And I said, "Thank you."

I went on to meet Prince Philip to congratulate him on his work in saving or rather trying to save some of the animals of Kenya, and I stood around until they were taken away.

I just thought she should know her connection to Fisk. And Fisk should know our connection to Royalty. I hope one day the Prince of Wales will come to visit us. And the Jubilee Singers will share the story of how their names changed to honor Victoria and why Jubilee Hall is called Jubilee Hall. And understand why the sound of the enslaved Americans is now the sound heard around the globe. Why Freedom is a song we created and sang for over two hundred years and why we still sing for all who seek it.

Nikki Giovanni
Class of 1965

COTTON IN THE ARMS OF THE MOUNTAINS

A gentle wind
Like a loving granddaughter
Combing
Her grandmother's hair
Carried her gift
To the beginning

We think it's ice
But really it's cotton
On the top of mountains
Built on the bones
Of those who came before

A gentle wind
Blew white hair
Off grandmothers
Up and up and up
Settling in the arms
Of grandfathers
Who were lynched
Or whipped
Or shot but always looking
At Grandmothers
To reflect in their eyes
The love

A gentle wind
Carrying the white hair
To the waiting
Arms

We call it glacial
We call it ice
We should call it
Cotton
resting in the arms
of our great mountains

WHERE WAS THE MUSIC

At First I thought
Of baths
A warm bath my grandmother
Would run
For me
Then rub my back
But No
This was angry
Running away from smiles
The water swept off
My feet
Pushed madly
Into the house
And I grabbed my grandmother's
Bible and my little dog
And climbed to the roof
To wait
For relief

I knew there was a moon
Up there
But I just couldn't hear
It sing

KEVIN POWELL 2020

I don't understand why the virus took
Over two hundred thousand people
But not trump and that third foreign woman

I do understand that republicans
Are cowards and so are those nazis
Cheering
And those kkk we now call police killing
Not to mention father and sons chasing unarmed Black men
and running their cars into crowds
Pretending they are brave or something

They are not only cowards
And nazis but evil fools
And who go to bed white
Wake up American
And hate themselves for having
To share this earth

They will not overcome
And we will not love them

I don't understand why
Biden doesn't know everytime
From Pilate and Lincoln and all the rest try
To forgive they are murdered
And I hope this is not the case

But what does 2020 mean to me

A chance to learn how to open oysters
Talk to friends
Catch up on my reading

Tell myself I am going to dust the house
Lie about it

Enjoy the cold weather coming in
Improve my hamburger making
(add a smidgen of nutmeg/fry slowly in butter)
Enjoy my own company not to mention football

And remember there will be tomorrow

Because there will be

And evil will go and good will come

I am Black
We have seen much worse

TEN DESCRIPTIONS OF ME

(For Mark Koplik)

01–I'm excited my latest book *Make Me Rain* is scheduled for October publication. That makes me happy because I am a jazz fan which is where the title comes from.

02–I guess the thing that really pleases me is I get to give a shout-out to Marvin Gaye on the cover photo. *What's Going On* had Gaye in the rain so I have a raincoat but the sky is blue.

03–I'm a big fan of Kwame Alexander and anything he is creating is well worth reading. I also love a young writer named Renée Watson. I have been reading and re-reading them.

04–If there were words of wisdom don't you think we all would know them by now? Oh, I guess I should say look out for the lies.

05–I call. The best part of the phone system now is you can call anyone anywhere. Do you know the young people don't even know what a party line is or that you had to pay for long distance?

06–I sincerely think you should fry your chicken slowly in butter. There is no rush. And do us all a favor: No Batter.

07–As the T-shirt says: Be Yourself. All others are taken.

08–I mostly dream.

09–I try to do my honest best with my poetry so I never try to choose. It would be like saying who is your favorite child.

10–I think life is interesting so I think we should enjoy living it. I guess the most important part is not learning to give love but learning to accept love.

Thanks for inviting me.

PROSE TO THE PEOPLE

We hear stories before we are born. Our mothers and, in fact, our grandmothers sing to us; sometimes Spirituals, sometimes jazz to keep our coming in rhythm with our ancestors. We are born and everyone who loves our family comes around to drink and eat and sing. We are happy. By the time we begin our own dreams we are given books with illustrations that we make up stories about. People give us books or money to buy books or paper to draw on and we make up our stories. Some of these stories are still with us. Some have been boxed away; some burned up; some simply thrown away but that's all right because there are libraries and bookstores.

Libraries are the university of the people. I loved going into the wood-floored green-lighted room where Index cards awaited. There was a world in those cards and I could pick any one of them I chose.

But then I learned how to drive and I could go to the bookstore. I could drive downtown, park, and go in looking grown-up. I always was neat; and I always spoke to the owners. I got to know the bookstore owners across America the same way I got to know my librarians.

I had an old clunker but gas was less than a dollar a gallon that I could drive from New York City to Detroit to Chicago to Denver to Portland then down the California coast meeting bookstore owners all the way. Coming back home was the southern route—Houston, Dallas, St. Louis, New Orleans, Mississippi, Cincinnati, Pittsburgh.

There were Black bookstores on almost every corner from Liberation Books to the famous and necessary National Memorial Bookstore to Vaughn's and my goodness did I leave Washington, DC, out? Every Black community had a Black bookstore. And we had pride. We had poetry. We had song. We had readings. Nothing was more important than the bookstores except perhaps the churches. The buildings have been taken but not forgotten. The songs are still being sung.

The Prose is still reminding us that "Black is Beautiful," as Mr. Michaux likes to say, "but knowledge is power."

POEMS

(For the Blacksburg Books Community Project)

Poems like the sunshine
Warm us
Like the moon
Make us fall in love
Like the stars twinkle
In our hearts
Like a creek
Ripples over fishes which we catch
Making us fall in love
Like the moon on a starry night
Or the sunshine on a spring morning.

Poems are a good idea.

WE HAVE PREVAILED

I want to take this minute to thank the Hokie Family for always being there to welcome me wherever I go to share my joy at being a part of our community. Whether on a ship cruising the European rivers or in London at the British Book Festival, in a small library in an Appalachian town or a coffee shop in New York the Hokies have welcomed me. And I always welcome them. As we are one. And we have prevailed.

WINTER HOMES

My goldfish are finding
winter homes under slabs
in the pond

Mother goldfish birthed
and hid four babies
this summer

they were not eaten
by birds
or their fathers

the heater is on

it's my contribution
to mother nature

I have aired my quilts
and washed my blankets

I will cuddle
with my dog
a good book and with any luck
a cup
of Frontier Soup

finding
my winter home

FATHERS

(For twg)

They all are handsome
Soft spoken
Laughing at your jokes
Giving a joke back

They didn't make
Any promises
Or money
But were pleasant
Enough
To be around

They had dreams
And hopes
Read maps
For places
They wanted
To visit

After walks
And movies
But not any
Promises

Except
        "It ain't mine"
Which was the only
Definite thing
They said

And off they went
Who knows where
To whom
For what

I and you have
This in common
We never saw
Them again

Not even in
Your smile
Or anger

Only
In your Blame

About the Author

NIKKI GIOVANNI (1943–2024), poet, activist, mother, grandmother, and educator, grew up in Tennessee and Ohio, and graduated with honors from Fisk University in Nashville. The author of more than thirty books, she was also the recipient of seven NAACP Image Awards, the Robert Frost Medal, the Langston Hughes Medal for Outstanding Poetry, an Emmy Award, and thirty-one honorary degrees. She garnered her most unusual honor in 2007 when a South American bat species—*Micronycteris giovanniae*—was named in celebration of her. A devoted teacher and honorary member of Delta Sigma Theta Sorority, Inc., Giovanni spent thirty-five years as University Distinguished Professor of English at Virginia Tech in Blacksburg, Virginia.